QILIN'S VOYAGE

Written by TANG YAMING
Illustrated by KOBAYASHI YUTAKA

Books Beyond Boundaries
ROYAL COLLINS

Over the course of 28 years, from the third year of the Yongle reign of the Ming Dynasty (AD 1405) to the eighth year of the Xuande reign (AD 1433), the Emperor dispatched Zheng He to lead a massive fleet. Commanding more than 200 ships and over 20,000 crew members, Zheng He embarked on seven grand voyages to the Western Seas, visiting over thirty countries across Asia and Africa—nearly a century before Columbus, creating a miraculous chapter in the annals of maritime history.

Our story unfolds during one of these monumental journeys undertaken by Zheng He's fleet.

Out on the vast ocean, the sailors battled fierce winds and towering waves daily. Just as their freshwater supplies neared depletion, and worry set in, a lookout spotted a line of red land where the sea met the sky. The great ships hastened toward this mysterious continent, drawing ever closer until the red soil and faint outlines of villages became visible. The crew was thrilled!

Zheng He's fleet had reached the Bay of Mombasa on the East African coast. Not far from the bay lay Paté Village, home to a young boy named Mosa.

Mosa, seven years old, would go to the grasslands daily with his father to herd cattle. While herding, Mosa enjoyed climbing the tall and cool acacia trees, and he could see into the distance. His best friends were two giraffes who came daily to nibble the acacia's branches.

Mosa named them "Tu Tu" and "Er Er."

Whenever Tu Tu and Er Er approached the acacia tree, Mosa would pick some tender branches and leaves to feed them. They would curl the leaves into their mouths with bluish-gray tongues, then blink at Mosa in gratitude. While stroking their protruding horns, Mosa would chat with them.

Each day after herding, Mosa would gather some dry grass and firewood to help his mother cook. His mother was soon to have another baby, and the thought of having a little brother or sister made Mosa's heart flutter with excitement.

That afternoon, Mosa's mother suddenly began to moan loudly, struggling in labor. The neighbor's aunt paced frantically by her bed.

The neighbor fetched Mosa's father, and the aunt said, "I've heard that the Chinese who came from the sea teach people to farm and even offer free medical care. Please, go and ask them for help!"

Mosa's father had never heard of China before, but with the dire situation, he hurried off.

When Mosa's father reached Mombasa Bay, he was stunned by the sight before him.

He had never seen so many large ships. The people disembarking looked different from the locals, with unfamiliar features and clothes.

Mosa's father couldn't worry about that now. Seeing the tribal elder talking with the strangers, he rushed over and shouted, "Help, please! My wife is having a difficult labor!"

Understanding the situation, Zheng He quickly summoned Lan Ma, a seamstress from his ship, to accompany Mosa's father to Paté Village.

Lan Ma, who also helped with midwifery among the locals during stops, rode a donkey provided by the elder to Mosa's home. Using traditional Chinese medicine techniques, she successfully helped Mosa's mother give birth.

The baby cried out, and Mosa danced with joy, exclaiming, "I have a little sister now!"

Time flew, and as word spread that Zheng He's fleet was preparing to return to China, villagers came to bid them farewell.

Mosa was puzzled to see his father and some uncles leading Tu Tu and Er Er toward the large ship.

The crew was loading food and goods onto the ship and were astonished to see the tall giraffes. The crew was amazed when the locals called them "kirin," thinking they were the mythical creatures known as qilin.

Mosa then learned that his father planned to give Tu Tu and Er Er to the people on the ship. He tearfully pleaded with his father, "I don't want to part with Tu Tu and Er Er!"

His father tried to console him, saying, "It's hard to catch other kirins quickly, and we were lucky to catch these two. These people are good; let's give them to them."

Hearing about the gift of two "qilin," Zheng He ordered silk, porcelain, and tea to be given in return.

Mosa followed his father, bringing Tu Tu and Er Er on the great ship. Everything was so new to him. The crew offered him freshly steamed buns to eat.

Tu Tu and Er Er were so tall that the crew had to let their necks stretch out through a skylight on the deck. Mosa had never seen them look like that and almost laughed aloud.

Thinking to himself, "I can't leave Tu Tu and Er Er," he sneaked into a pile of feed and hay in the ship's hold, staying silent.

As the horn sounded, Zheng He's fleet set sail.
Mosa's father, not seeing Mosa and thinking he had already disembarked, left the ship amid tears and laughter from those waving goodbye.
Goodbye, goodbye!

The ship gradually quieted down.
 Rocked by the gentle sway of the great ship, Mosa lay nestled in a soft pile of hay and unknowingly drifted off to sleep. After some time, he awoke in the dim light.
 Hearing Tu Tu and Er Er munching on grass, he suddenly felt hungry.

Suddenly, he saw a pair of green eyes staring at him—it was a calico cat. The cat meowed softly and walked away.

Mosa tried to close his eyes and sleep again, but sleep eluded him. He began to think of home, of his father, mother, and his newly born sister, sure that his family must be searching for him everywhere.

Mosa started to cry softly, regretting his decision to hide on the ship.

As sunlight streamed through the skylight into the cabin, Mosa rubbed his eyes.

Suddenly, he saw someone smiling at him—it was Lan Ma, the midwife who had helped his mother.

"Ah, here you are! My kitty didn't deceive me!" Lan Ma exclaimed as she pulled Mosa out from the hay.

Lan Ma took Mosa to her cabin, brought him some hot water, and handed him steamed buns and stir-fried bean sprouts.

She sighed, "Oh, dear child, you're quite pitiful, stuck far from home. We had to leave some sick crew members in Mombasa, and like you, they can't go home either."

Mosa didn't understand Lan Ma's words but kept nodding as he stuffed his mouth with buns.

Lan Ma hid Mosa in her room and began teaching him a few Chinese phrases daily.

One day, Mosa was discovered. The crew brought him before Zheng He.

Zheng He asked the trembling boy, "I hear you're from Paté village. Why are you hiding on the ship?"

Mosa could only repeat, "My kirin! The buns are tasty!" Zheng He laughed heartily.

"Since you followed your qilin here, I will take you to the great Ming Emperor with us. But you must take good care of the qilin, ensuring they survive the journey, okay?"

It seemed Mosa understood as he nodded vigorously.

From that day, Mosa took care of Tu Tu and Er Er, feeding them, cleaning them, and keeping them company.

But the giraffes were sensitive and timid; confined to the ship, they grew thinner daily. Mosa was at a loss.

A crew member advised him, "Aren't the qilin your good friends? Talk to them, cheer them up."

Mosa thought, "Yes, indeed! Tu Tu and Er Er are in a strange place; they need my comfort."

He spent each day petting the long necks of Tu Tu and Er Er, trying his best to keep them happy. He showed them the blue sky and the seabirds and told them about all the new things he was seeing on the ship . . .

Mosa scattered some dried meat to attract seabirds onto the deck, engaging playfully with Tu Tu and Er Er. The giraffes stretched out their long tongues, warmly greeting the seabirds.

With Mosa's careful care and companionship, his "qilin" gradually regained their spirits.

The crew told Mosa, "Seeing seabirds means land is not far away."

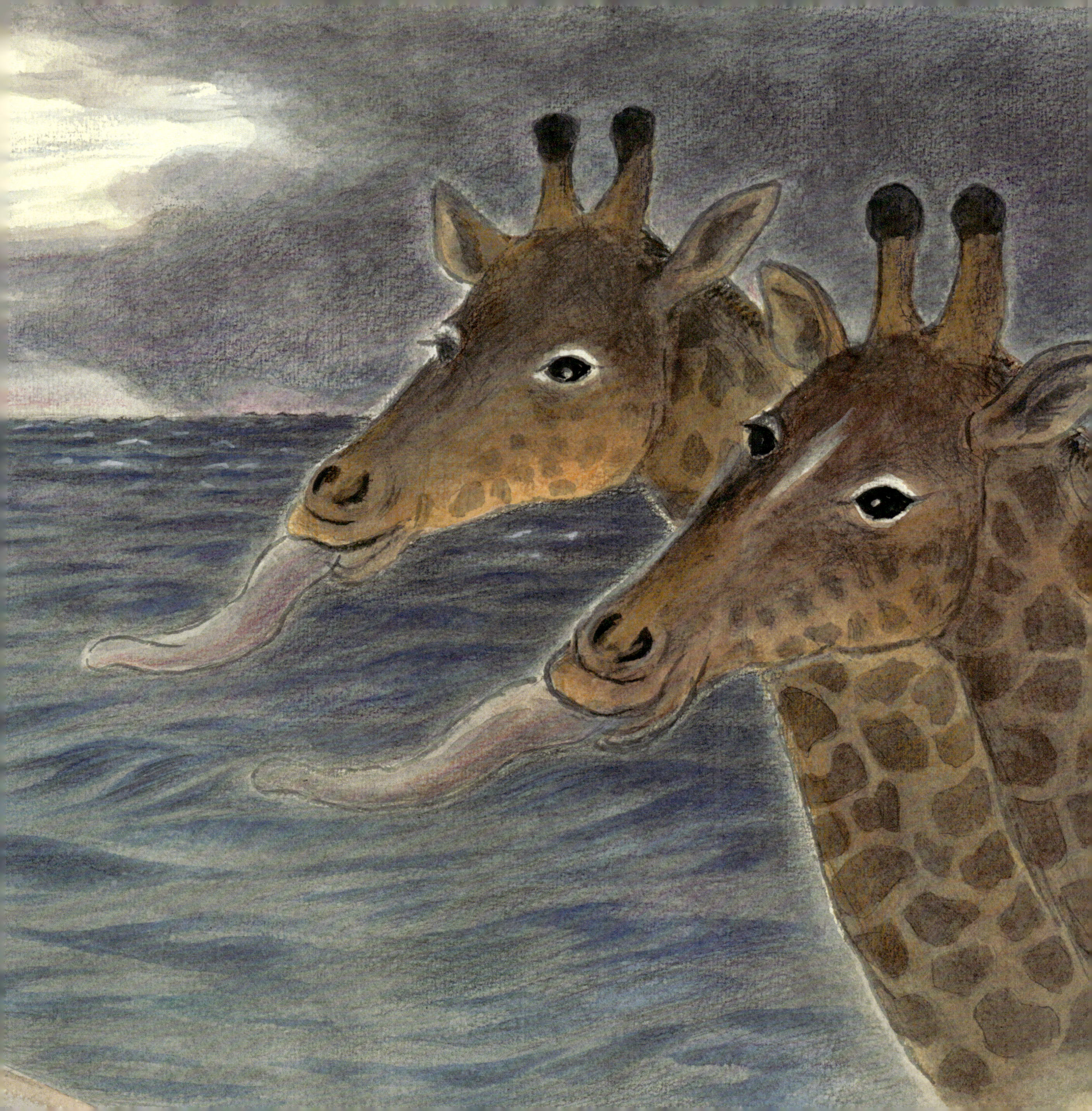

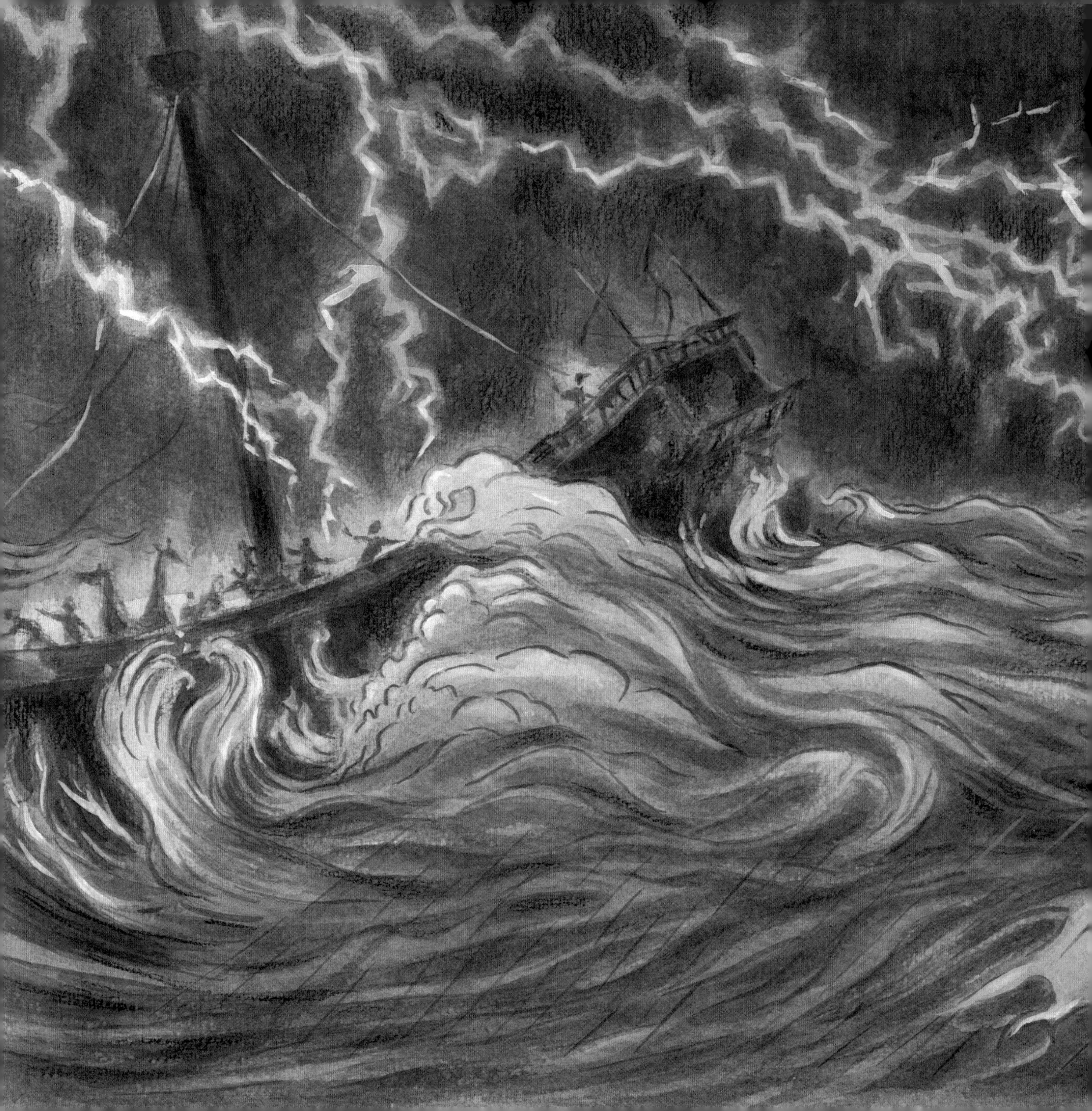

One stormy night, a typhoon struck, with lightning flashing and rain pouring down. The ship rocked violently, nearly being swallowed by the monstrous waves.

Tu Tu and Er Er struggled to stand, their heads on the deck battered by the massive waves, gasping for air. Mosa and the crew braced against the storm, securing wooden frames and canvas around their heads to allow them to breathe.

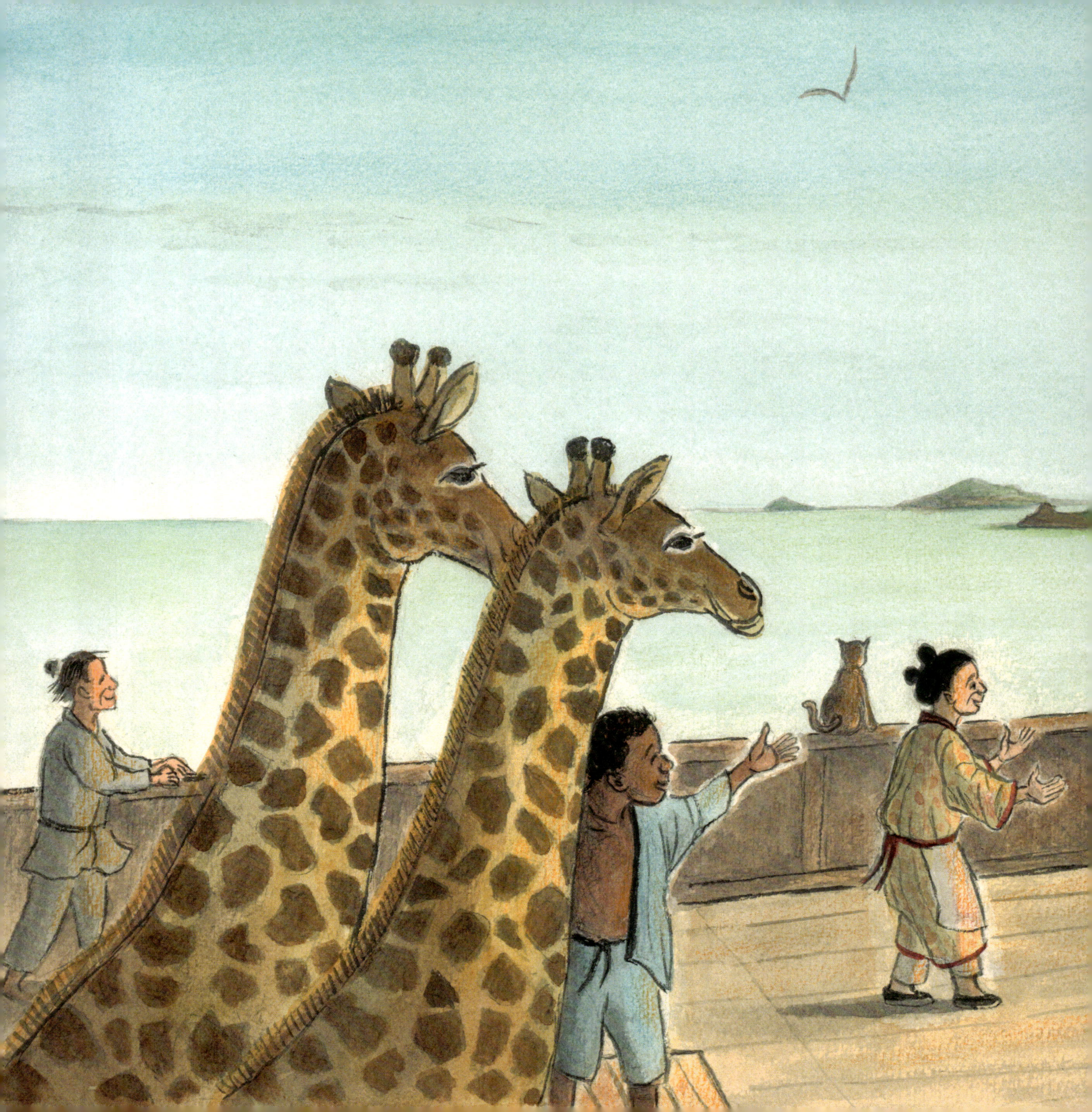

After the storm cleared, Mosa saw land in the distance.
"There lie the islands of the great Ming!" cheered the crew as they rushed onto the deck, with Lan Ma and her calico cat joining them.

Tears streaming down his face, Mosa stroked Tu Tu and Er Er, who blinked back at him continuously.

The fleet sped forward, heading toward their long-missed homeland.

Zheng He's fleet arrived at Liujiagang in Jiangsu Province, where a grand welcoming ceremony was held. The shore was crowded, with drums beating loudly as they greeted the returning fleet.

As the crew disembarked, they embraced their families, crying and laughing, jumping and bouncing with joy.

Mosa, following Lan Ma, had never seen such a grand scene and clung tightly to her hand, afraid of getting lost.

People on the shore gathered around Tu Tu and Er Er, eager to see what the "qilin" actually looked like.

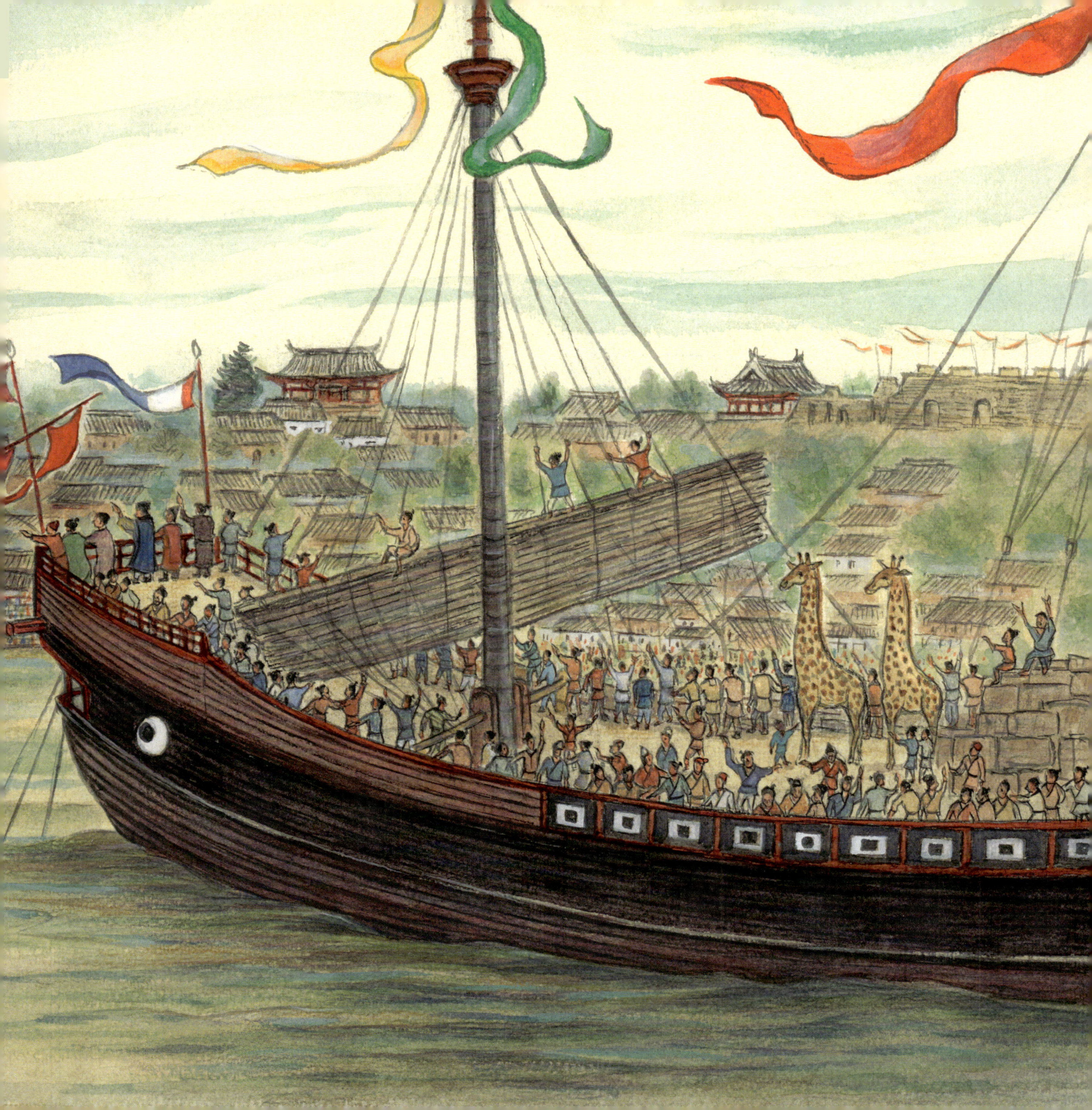

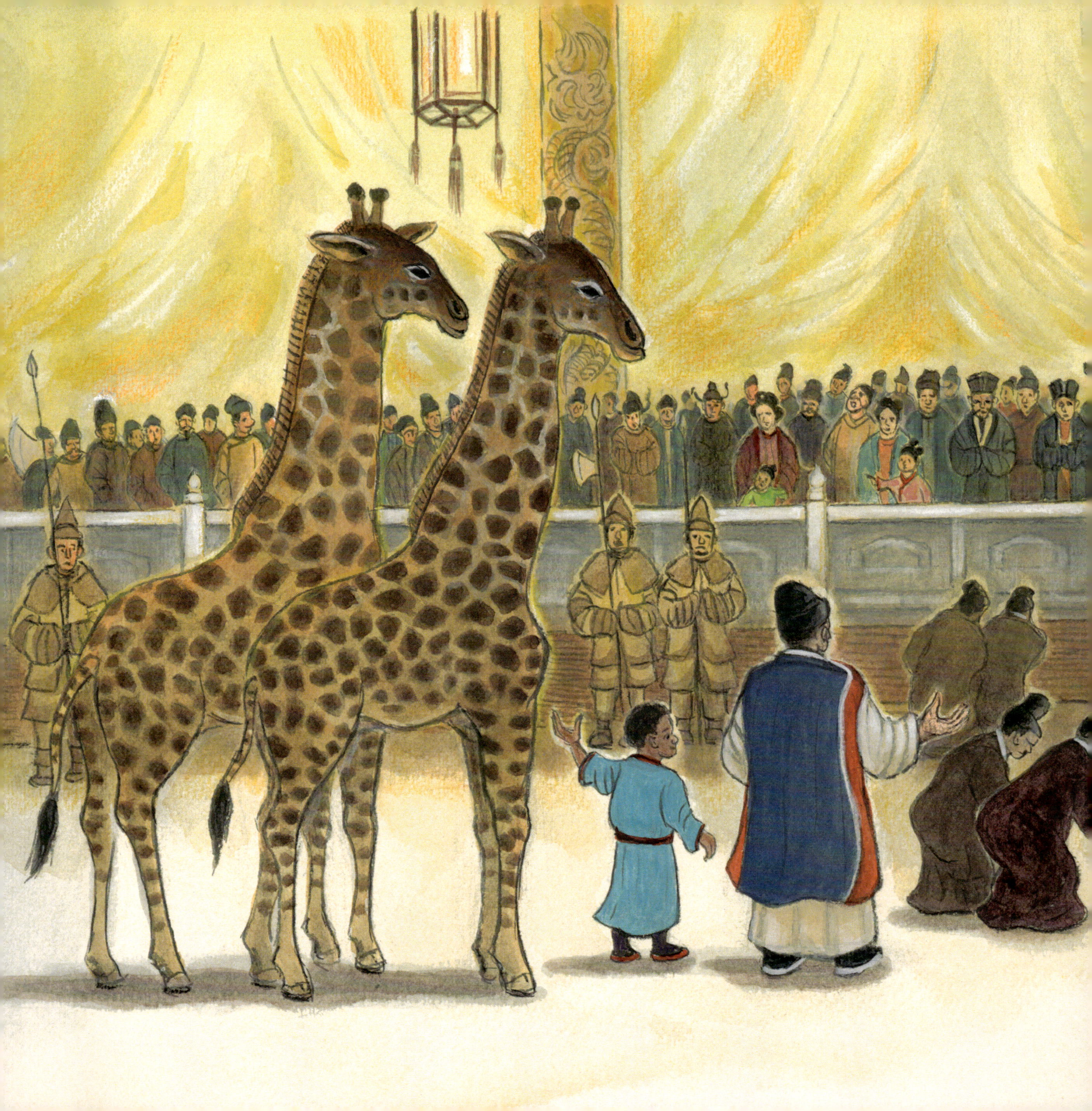

Zheng He led Mosa, along with Tu Tu and Er Er, to the Imperial Palace in Nanjing.

Yongle Emperor happily stroked Mosa's head, looked up at the giraffes, and said, "Ah, these are the qilin, symbols of good fortune and peace, emblems of a prosperous era!"

Thus, Mosa and his "qilin" stayed in the great Ming. Over six hundred years have passed, and Mosa's descendants have long become members of the Chinese people.

The descendants of Zheng He's crew who stayed in Africa came to study in Nanjing and were warmly welcomed.

Children in China can now see lovely African giraffes in zoos nationwide.

Today, the China-aided Mombasa to Nairobi railway in Kenya features numerous wildlife crossings, allowing giraffes to pass without bending down.

In the long flow of history, the touching stories of friendship between the Chinese and African peoples are endless.

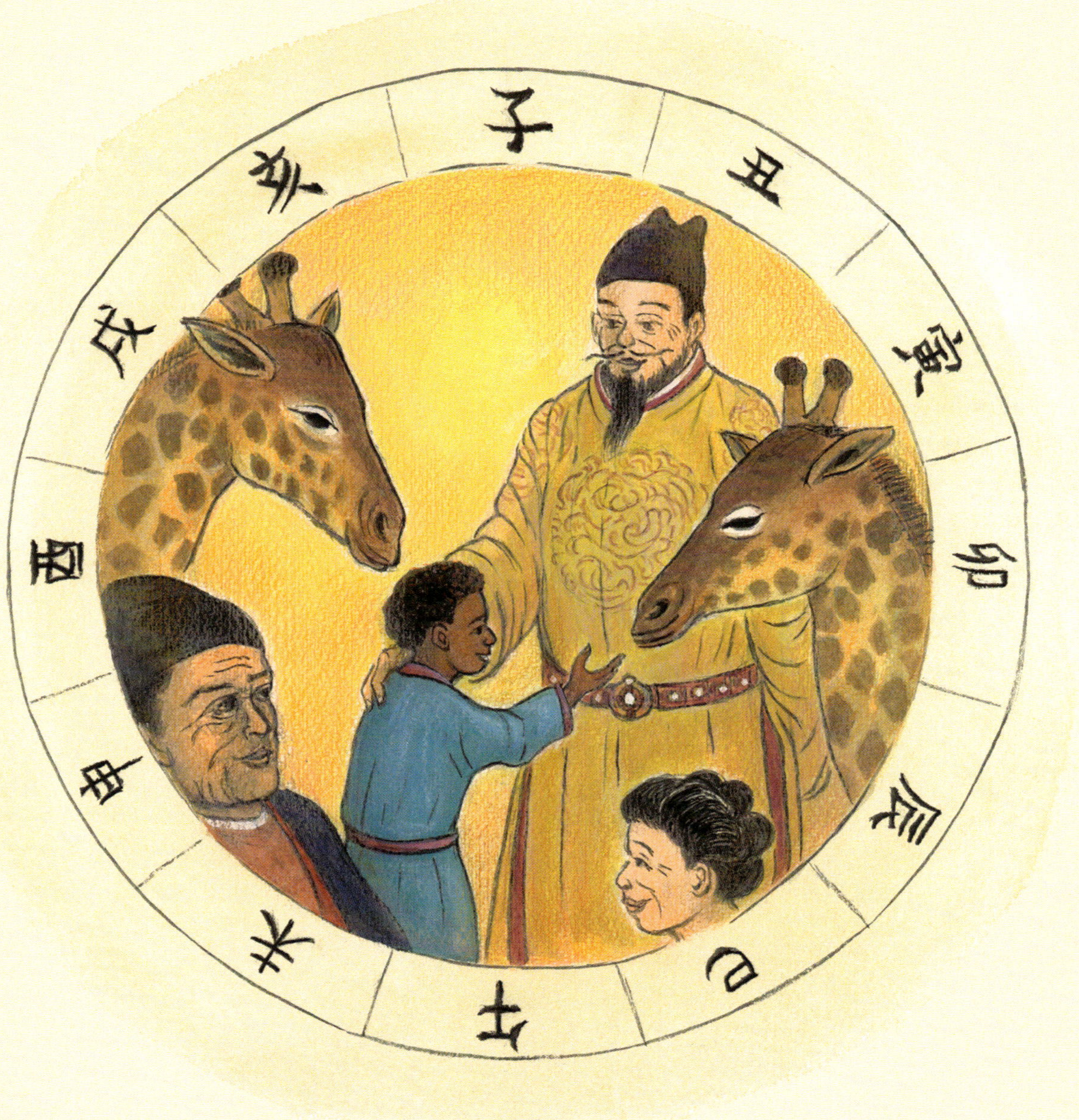
子
丑
寅
卯
辰
巳
午
未
申
酉
戌
亥

Cultural Notes

Zheng He: A famous Chinese mariner, explorer, diplomat, and fleet admiral during the early Ming Dynasty. He is known for his seven long voyages promoting trade and diplomatic relations between China and countries in Asia and Africa.

Qilin: In Chinese mythology, the qilin is a mythical hooved creature known as a symbol of good luck. It is often depicted with dragon-like features. Historically, the term was sometimes used to describe giraffes brought back to China from Africa during Zheng He's voyages.

Treasure Ship: Large wooden ships were used during Zheng He's voyages. These ships were among the largest and most advanced of their time and were used for carrying goods, treasures, and emissaries over long distances.

Mombasa Bay: A natural harbor and major maritime center on the east coast of Africa, one of the stops by Zheng He's fleet.

Paté Village: A fictional small village near Mombasa Bay, where Mosa, a young local boy, lives.

Midwife: A person trained to assist in childbirth. In *Qilin's Voyage*, midwives aboard Zheng He's ships also help locals with their medical needs, showing knowledge exchange between cultures.

Yongle Emperor (Zhu Di, also known as Emperor Chengzu of Ming): The third emperor of the Ming Dynasty, under whose reign Zheng He conducted his voyages. Known for his ambition to expand Chinese maritime and commercial influence.

Ocean's Emotion, Journey's Expanse, and the Strength of Humanity

Tang Yaming

I was born in Beijing, far from any sea. My only experience with the sea before the age of seven was a family vacation to the coastal city of Beidaihe, a memory that has stayed with me my entire life. As I grew older, my encounters with the sea became more frequent. I later lived on an island nation and had opportunities to travel to various countries, seeing most of the world's seas, including the Aegean, Caribbean, Baltic, Red, Black, and Dead Seas. Whenever the sea appears before me, I can't help but feel my heart surge and feel the urge to shout aloud. Even if I can't swim in it, I must touch the water, letting the cool sea dampen my skin.

There's an inexplicable longing humans have for the sea. Scientists say that, ultimately, humanity emerged from the sea—this I wholly believe. The amniotic fluid in our mothers' wombs, the newborn's instinct to hold their breath underwater, the salt we consume every day—all connect our imaginations and emotions to the sea, which is fundamental to human survival.

In elementary school, I learned about the great feats of Zheng He, who ventured into the Western Seas seven times over 600 years ago. Today, I am comforted that I can turn these stories into picture books for children. Now, I would like to gather some information about fascinating aspects that didn't quite make it into the picture book.

1. Did Zheng He's Fleet Circumnavigate the Globe?

Gavin Menzies, a retired officer of the British Royal Navy, spent 15 years visiting over 200 medieval-era famous ports and researching in over 900 libraries across more than 100 countries, looking for records and historical relics related to Zheng He. In his book, *1421: The Year China Discovered America*, he argues that the Ming Dynasty's naval capabilities were 300 years ahead of Europe's. He believes that Zheng He's fleet not only visited Southeast Asia, the Indian Ocean, and Africa but also circumnavigated the world.

Zheng He embarked on his first voyage 87 years before Columbus, 92 years before Vasco da Gama, and 116 years before Magellan reached the Philippines. At its peak, his fleet consisted of 200–300 ships with up to 28,000 crew members. The flagship, known as the "Treasure Ship," weighed over 1,000 tons—several times larger than Columbus's flagship on his voyage to the New World.

After Zheng He's seventh voyage, the Ming Dynasty strictly prohibited oceanic voyages and ceased the building of long-distance ships, punishing violators with death, and most of the navigational records were destroyed. However, Menzies believes that some of the navigational charts and celestial maps drawn by Zheng He's fleet were taken by the Italian merchant Niccolò de' Conti, who boarded a Chinese ship in India and later brought these maps back to Venice. These were then used by European navigators like da Gama, Magellan, and Cook, and some of these maps are still preserved in museums worldwide.

Following Zheng He, China's maritime ventures declined, pirates began to ravage China's coastlines, and China entered an era of seclusion. Meanwhile, maritime trade and the Industrial Revolution propelled the West into modernity.

Though there is still debate over whether Zheng He's fleet truly circumnavigated the globe, Menzies's theory continues to excite me deeply.

2. Did Zheng He's Fleet Leave Crew Members in Africa?

In 1998, an American journalist visited Paté Island in Kenya's Lamu Archipelago and unexpectedly heard that the local Famao people claimed to be descendants of the Chinese. Finding this intriguing, the journalist reported on it, sparking international interest. Subsequently, scholars conducted archaeological studies on Paté Island, uncovering many fragments of ancient Chinese porcelain around the Famao settlements. This discovery led to further media interest, including reports from Xinhua News Agency.

It is said that many Famao people share the surname "Wei," which sounds like the Chinese surnames "魏" or "卫." The most direct evidence came from a DNA test in 2002. The test results of a 63-year-old Famao woman confirmed she indeed had Chinese ancestry. Later, her daughter received a scholarship to study traditional Chinese medicine in China.

The legends of the Famao people about the arrival of the Chinese on Paté Island align precisely with the time Zheng He's fleet reached the East African coast, suggesting the Famao are likely descendants of survivors from Zheng He's fleet who were shipwrecked. In Portuguese, Famao means "one who has escaped death from the sea." Legends among the Famao tell of about twenty Chinese who encountered a shipwreck hundreds of years ago and were washed ashore on Paté Island. These skilled Chinese helped the local tribes by killing a giant python that had plagued the island for years, earning the elders' trust and permission to settle there. While most did not wish to stay, eventually only six remained. These six married local women and had children, thus founding the Famao community. The Famao people have slightly yellowish skin tones and facial features that resemble the Chinese, distinguishing them from their neighbors.

Additionally, in *When China Ruled the Seas* (Guangxi Normal University Press, 2004), author Li Luye shares her experiences in Kenya. She met people on Bardi Island who claimed they were descendants of Chinese shipwreck survivors from centuries ago. Li wrote about Bardi Island, a remote area in northern Kenya covered in dense jungles without electricity or roads. The residents of Kenda and Faza villages have features that hint at Asian ancestry—eyes, hair, and skin tone. Later, in Xiyu Village, she met a fisherman in his forties named Badu, who caught her attention with his light skin and slightly slanted eyes. After a while, Li asked about his background. "I'm from the Famao tribe. We have about 50 or 100 people here. Legend has it we are descendants of Chinese or others." He continued, "Many years ago, a Chinese ship ran aground here, and the sailors swam ashore to what we now call Shangjia Village, marrying local women, which is why we Famao look different."

Another Famao man with slightly Asian features approached to listen. His name was Michi, and he also shared an early story of a Chinese shipwreck told by elders. He even revealed something astonishing: Africans had given giraffes to the Chinese in the past. The next day, Li met a 55-year-old Famao man named Bonnahuei, who proudly told her, "My ancestors were Chinese or Vietnamese or something like that."

According to records such as the *Veritable Records of Emperor Chengzu of Ming*, on his fourth voyage, Zheng He passed through the Indian Ocean to the Strait of Hormuz and the Arabian Peninsula, presenting silk and gems in Mecca. Zheng He, originally surnamed Ma, came from the Hui (Muslim) ethnic group in Yunnan, and visiting Mecca was a dream held by his ancestors for generations.

Furthermore, Zheng He's fleet discovered a type of animal with an extremely long neck on the East African coast, which the Somalis called "kirin," thinking these were the mythical unicorns, or "qilin." The crew, excited, loaded several giraffes onto their ships as gifts for Yongle Emperor. The fact that villagers on distant Bardi Island knew of this ancient history of giraffes being sent to China is unimaginable unless the Chinese sailors had passed down the giraffe story through generations.

Most of the pottery found in Famao households on Bardi Island indicates inheritance, not trade. Li also visited ancient Famao graves, which resembled Chinese hill tombs. Researchers found that craftsmen on Bardi and Bamo Islands weave baskets in a style common to Southern China, a craft not found in mainland Kenya. The drums on Bardi Island resemble those used by the Chinese, and some local dialect words might originate from Chinese. Shockingly, in 1569, the Portuguese missionary Monclaro wrote that Bardi Island had a thriving silk production industry, unique in Kenya. Several elderly residents told Li that their island once produced silk until about 50 years ago.

3. Were There Women on Zheng He's Fleet?

In ancient China, women were generally forbidden to be aboard ships. The prevailing belief was that women on board brought bad luck, as they supposedly carried a "heavy *yin* energy" unfavorable for sailing. This superstition stemmed from feudal attitudes that prioritized men over women.

However, in the fleet of Zheng He, who was a eunuch, there were indeed women. There were two types of women in the fleet: seamstresses and midwives. During Zheng He's voyages, which could last several years and involve hundreds of ships and over 20,000 crew members, many wore fabric shoes and socks. These older women seamstresses were responsible for sewing and repairing clothes and footwear for the crew.

The other group consisted of midwives. Zheng He's missions included spreading advanced Chinese civilization, embodying the mission to "transform the barbarian customs with rituals and teachings." In those times, many countries lacked advanced medical techniques, particularly in midwifery, which often resulted in the deaths of both mothers and babies. Therefore, Zheng He's ships carried two midwives who would teach local populations midwifery skills wherever they went. The fleet also set up tents for medical consultations and treatment, disseminating medical knowledge. These benevolent acts were highly regarded by the local populations.

Zheng He's fleet also included Taoist priests and entertainers, who were responsible for the crew's spiritual welfare.

Although some of this information cannot be verified and may not be entirely accurate, it has inspired me creatively. The publication of *Qilin's Voyage* would not have been possible without the strong support of the Changjiang Children's Press (Group) Ltd. When I first proposed creating this book, colleagues such as He Long, Liu Jiapeng, Chen Ying, and Luo Man provided immense help by facilitating access to extensive resources, verifying historical facts, and revising the manuscript multiple times. The picture book took three years to complete.

This book also owes much to the renowned Japanese picture book artist Kobayashi Yutaka, whose dedication has always inspired me. His picture books have been translated into many languages for Chinese readers, but this was his first time creating specifically for them. I got to know him while working as a picture book editor at Fukuinkan in Japan. He readily agreed to illustrate this for the children of China. Kobayashi has visited China several times. To prepare for this book, he read extensively and frequently visited libraries to research maps and other materials, showing a true craftsman's dedication to his work.

I remember once a British friend asked me, "Your Chinese fleets visited so many countries so early on; why didn't you claim some territories?" I didn't know how to answer then, but I simply said that China and Britain are different; China has never been an aggressor, and the Chinese aspire to "universal harmony."

When I was young, the Beijing Zoo was close to home, and the African giraffes were one of my favorite animals to watch. Also, I loved poems and stories about the sea from a young age and enjoyed singing songs about the ocean. They always brought me fantasies and impulses. Having lived more than half my life and seen so many seas, I deeply feel that the real sea and the sea of dreams cannot be spoken of in the same breath. Ask any fisherman by the sea, and you'll know—the real sea has a cruel, indifferent, and merciless side. Only those who bravely contend with the sea have a chance to survive.

I never imagined that my childhood love for giraffes and fascination with the sea would one day evolve into a picture book. I want to take this opportunity to tell the children: Your dreams will surely blossom and bear fruit once they find the right soil. Embrace and nurture your aspirations and passions!

The sea has emotions, connecting China with the world; the journey is long, and only those who do not fear the raging waves and storms can reach the other shore; the strength of people, through countless generations and numerous struggles, will surely achieve the great rejuvenation of the Chinese nation!

Zheng He

Zheng He (1371/1375–1433/1435) was a Ming Dynasty explorer and mariner. Originally named Ma and sometimes called Wen He, with the courtesy name Sanbao, he was from the Hui ethnic group in Kunyang, Yunnan (now Jinning). He entered the imperial palace in the early Ming Dynasty, served under Prince Yan, and was granted the surname Zheng. In 1405, during the third year of the Yongle reign, he commanded a fleet to the Western Seas, returning after two years. Over a span of 28 years, he conducted seven voyages, visiting over thirty countries and regions, reaching as far as the East African coast and the Red Sea. These voyages promoted economic and cultural exchanges between China and the countries of Asia and Africa. After his sixth voyage, he served as the commander of the Nanjing garrison. He died on his way back from his last voyage and was buried at the foot of Mount Niushou in Nanjing. Some sources suggest he died in 1435 in Nanjing. (From *Cihai*)

Zheng He's Voyages to the Western Seas

The voyages Zheng He led are considered to be monumental achievements in the history of long-distance navigation. Starting in 1405, Emperor Chengzu sent Zheng He, along with deputy Wang Jinghong, and a crew of 27,800 people aboard 62 treasure ships to sail the Western Seas—a term that referred to the ocean west of Brunei at that time. The fleet set sail from Liujiagang in Suzhou (now Dongliuhe Town, Jiangsu) and visited places like Champa (southern Vietnam today), Java, Sumatra, and Ceylon (Sri Lanka), then returned via the west coast of India by 1407. Further voyages took place from 1407 to 1409, 1409 to 1411, 1413 to 1415, 1417 to 1419, 1421 to 1422 (all during the Yongle reign), and 1431 to 1433 (during the Xuande reign), making a total of seven voyages over 28 years that reached the East African coast, the Red Sea, and the Islamic holy city of Mecca. The largest ships in his fleet were 44 *zhang* and four *chi* (approximately 444 feet) long, and 18 *zhang* (approximately 180 feet) wide, accommodating a thousand people. These voyages occurred over half a century before those of Columbus, da Gama, and others, with the size and scale of his fleet far surpassing theirs. Zheng He exchanged goods like porcelain, silk, and metals for local products, strengthening ties with countries throughout Southeast Asia. Many places in Southeast Asia still retain relics from Zheng He's voyages. (From *Cihai*)

Zheng He's Treasure Ships and Fleet

To undertake these voyages, Zheng He built what were then the largest sailing ships in the world, known as the "Treasure Ships," totaling 62 vessels. Besides the treasure ships, his fleet included numerous other ships, with a total crew exceeding 20,000 people.

About the Author

TANG YAMING was born in Beijing. He has worked as an editor for the *China Tourism Newspaper* and a translator of Japanese songs for the Chinese Musicians' Association. In 1983, at the invitation of Tadashi Matsui, known as the "father of picture books" in Japan, Tang entered the renowned Japanese children's publishing house, Fukuinkan Shoten. There, he became the first non-Japanese official editor in the Japanese publishing industry, where he was active for 35 years, editing a large number of excellent books and receiving various awards both domestically and internationally.

His main works include the essay collection *Cherry Blossom Sentiments · Panda Troubles* (Iwanami Shoten), the novel *Jade Dew* (TBS, which won the eighth Kaiji Ken Award), the travelogue *Walking in Tokyo* (China Tourism Publishing House), the picture book *Nezha Conquers the Sea* (which won the 22nd Kodansha Publishing Culture Award), and *Journey to the West* (which won the 48th Sanei Children's Publishing Culture Award) (all published by Kodansha).

His major translations include *Building Bridges* by Empress Michiko of Japan (Juvenile & Children's Publishing), Yoko Sano's *The Cat Who Lived a Million Times* (Jieli Publishing House), and Jiang Rong's *Wolf Totem* and *Little Wolf, Little Wolf* (all published by Kodansha).

He has authored and translated over 100 works in Chinese and Japanese. Tang graduated from Waseda University and the Graduate School of the University of Tokyo. He has long worked at NHK, engaging in broadcast translation and scriptwriting, and has taught at Toyo University, Waseda University, and Sophia University. He has served as a director of the Japanese Board on Books for Young People (JBBY), a juror for the Bologna Book Fair's Illustrators' Exhibition, and a judge for the Feng Zikai Chinese Children's Picture Book Award. Currently, he is the honorary president of the Federation of Literary and Art Circles of Overseas Chinese in Japan and a director of the Japanese Chinese Professors Association. In recent years, he has edited, translated, created, and published many picture books in China.

Tang Yaming

About the Illustrator

KOBAYASHI YUTAKA was born in Tokyo and graduated from Rikkyo University with a degree in Sociology. During his studies in the United Kingdom, he resolved to become a painter. From the 1970s to the 1980s, he traveled extensively throughout the Middle East and Asia, trekking, riding trains, carriages, bicycles, camels, and donkeys. During these journeys across deserts where water and food were scarce, he enjoyed interacting with innocent children fascinated by this foreigner. He believes that "the sparks that fly from personal interactions are more powerful than words and bring warmth to the heart." These experiences later became significant themes in his creative work.

His major picture book titles include *The Most Beautiful Village in the World—My Hometown* (winner of the 1996 Sanei Children's Publishing Culture Award and the Fuji Television Award), *The Circus Comes to Town* (selected for the 1997 National Youth Book Review Competition), *Our Day on the Street*, *Little Mountain* (both published by Shirakaba), *My Chopardiz* (Mitsumura Educational Books), and the series *Walking with My Brother* (Iwasaki Bookstore), *Cherry Blossom City* (Kosei Publishing), and *Yodogawa Story: The Day the Ship Came* (Iwanami Shoten). He has also written essays such as *Why War Cannot End—What I Saw and Heard in Afghanistan*.

His most famous picture book, *The 36th Parallel North*, features him as a giant bird that sets out from Tokyo in the evening and flies along the 36th parallel north, passing through Gyeongju in South Korea, Xi'an in China, the deserts of Afghanistan, the plateaus of Iran, the straits of Turkey, and finally reaching the Strait of Gibraltar.

Kobayashi Yutaka

Qilin's Voyage

Tang Yaming
Illustrations by Kobayashi Yutaka
Translated by Wu Meilian

First published in 2025 by Royal Collins Publishing Group Inc.
Groupe Publication Royal Collins Inc.
550-555 boul. René-Lévesque O Montréal (Québec) H2Z1B1 Canada

Original edition © Changjiang Children's Press (Group) Ltd.

All rights reserved. Without limiting the rights under copyright reserved above, no part of this publication may be reproduced, stored in or introduced into a retrieval system, or transmitted in any form or by any means (electronic, mechanical, photocopying, recording, or otherwise), without the prior written permission of both the copyright owner and the above publisher of this book.

ISBN: 978-1-4878-1271-3

To find out more about our publications, please visit www.royalcollins.com.

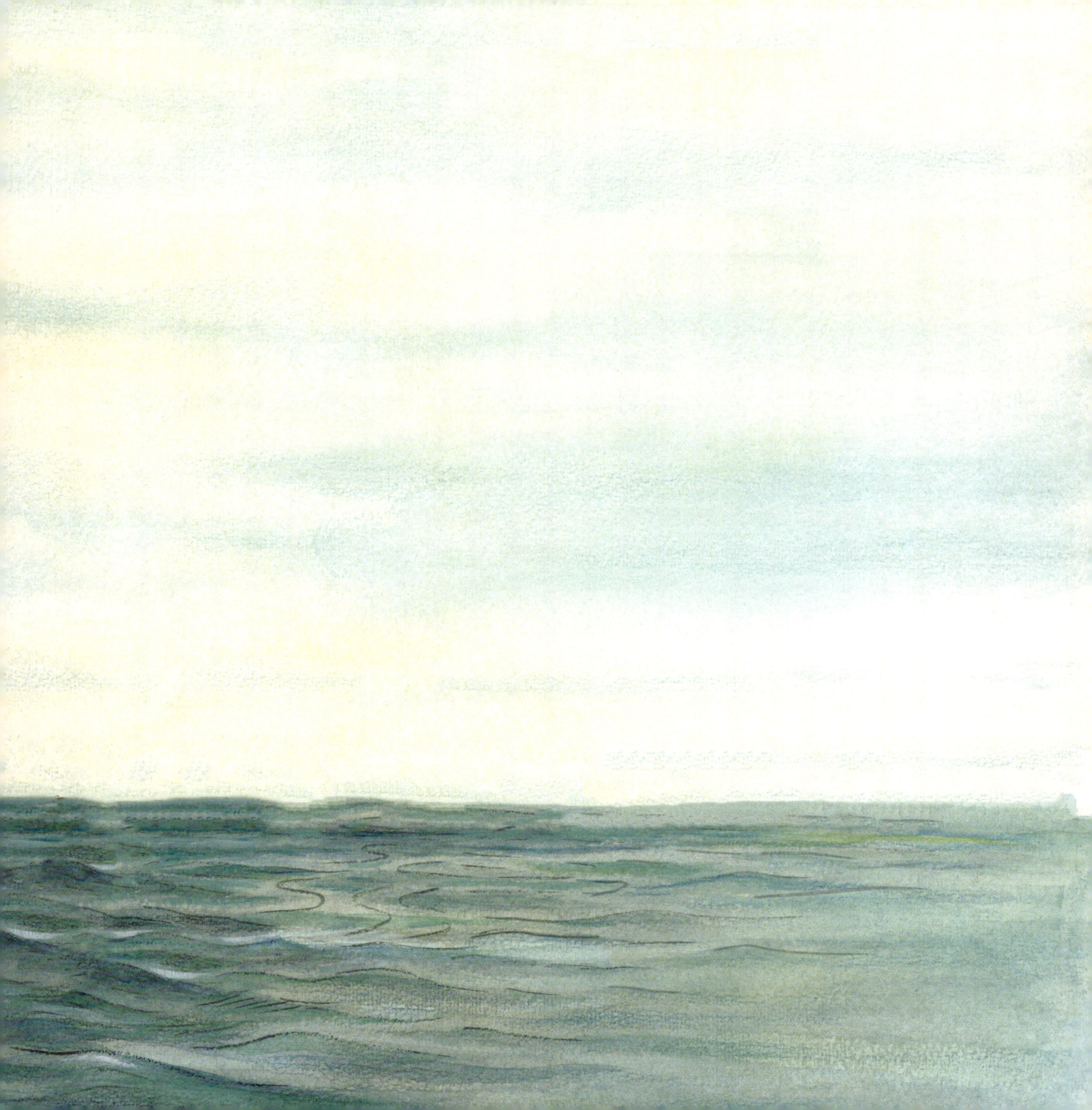

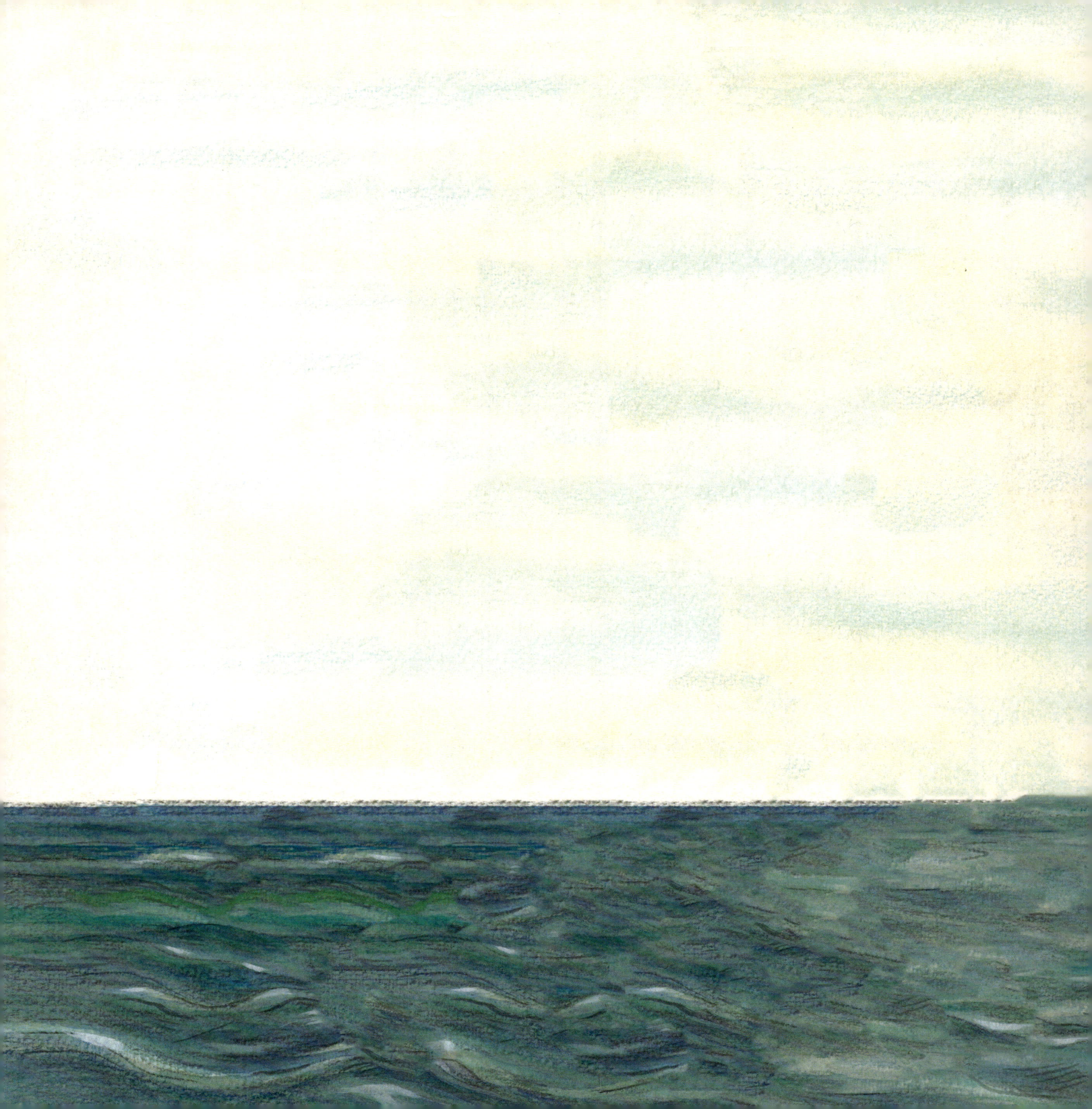